Santa Breaks Bad

An international Christmas story
wrapped in flash

Jodi Barnes

Cover Photo:

George Tsartsianidis/Santa Claus Is Not Coming This Year/Photos.com

ISBN: 0615911471
ISBN-13: 978-0615911472

For JB

Special thanks to Sarah, Rae, Tina, Tom and Jabs.

You Better Watch Out

It was bound to happen. Even celebrities can only take so much. The constant comparisons to Christ (people still think He was born in December), assumptions that he was anti-Semite or anti-Islam, and accusations from PETA, now ad litem for the reindeer. His credit rating was at an all time low.

Global warming had ruined the sleigh's optimal flight patterns long before Al Gore inconvenienced much of the world. Reluctantly, Santa began to outsource in the late eighties, after the elves took early retirement in droves. Those who remained spoke of collective bargaining, which almost broke his heart.

Still, Santa made good on his promise of lifetime healthcare and a Rolex for 30 years of service, although the watches were now shipped from China under the brand *Roll-X*. Given his integrity in other matters, he didn't think the elves would mind.

But they did. His remaining helpers – a vote soon taken to switch their identity to *Master Crafters* – posted photos of Che Guevara and Norma Rae throughout the Village.

They planned their own Christmas party to which he was never invited.

That was about the time things began to go south with Mrs. Claus, her fur-lined coat and spectacles abandoned for a pantsuit and contacts. By the end of the millennium, she sported Liz Claiborne jeans. Two years ago, she jammed herself into jeggings, thanks to Jenny Craig and FedEx.

She stopped making cookies in 2007.

With her latest nip-tuck, Mrs. Claus looks like the Joker. In fact, word on the Iceberg is she gets chemical peels at Joker's flagship spa. The two were recently spotted at a Lady Gaga concert in Dubai, but even Pinko, the Master Crafters' chief steward, can't bring himself to tell Santa.

Santa stands in the layaway line at TJ Maxx to pay down a $525 billion tab. The odds of getting Christmas out of hock by the 24th are close to zero unless he dies, so he tries not to think about it. He has little faith that Mrs. Claus would use his death benefit to pay off the layaway and hire a competent, caring successor. Last month, Blitzen suggested Kickstarter, but Santa never learned to type.

The woman in front of him drops what sounds like a coin onto the dirty floor. Santa bends down. On his way back up with a penny, he groans. The result is an audible "Ho." He holds the penny out to her but his back isn't cooperating. He inadvertently pokes her ample bottom, unable to be anything but eye level with its jiggly girth and then her crotch as she whips around.

"What the *hell*? Oh, no you didn't!" Her bejeweled hand

knocks the coin back to the floor. He manages to straighten his posture. He recognizes her from Mrs. Claus' reality TV binge, circa 2009.

"Oh, no. I didn't mean—"

"Save it, fat boy," Snooki's laugh commands each follicle on his neck and back to stand at attention. *He's not in Jersey. Is he in Jersey? Why is he in Jersey?*

She jerks back around, whipping his rosy cheeks with deep purple hair extensions.

While he should grant her a modicum of the charity he eagerly distributes across the world – despite rumors and fears, despite the need for cultural heroes and scapegoats, despite boring husbands, militant elves, and the frustration that nobody seems to accept altruism as its own reward – he steps back and swings his big black boot into her bulbous backside.

Snooki only wobbles like those egg-shaped, bottom-heavy toys he delivered in the seventies, *but* – he marvels – *she don't fall down!*

He grabs her baby carrier and a Neiman Marcus bag next to it without thinking.

"My stuff!" Snooki screams.

Santa runs out of line and into Housewares where he spies a butcher-block knife display. He removes the largest handle and points its blade at a woman in a shiny blue security jacket chugging toward him, a comely locomotive, puffing with purpose. Although he signals for her to stop by slicing the air, her forearm rises up and meets the blade.

He winces and changes direction, brandishing the blood-tipped knife like a charging knight. Santa is blinded by adrenaline and unwrapped rage. He looks downright giddy as he exits through the Enter Only door.

Before he hoists himself onto his sleigh, he remembers the baby carrier, looks down. It's a boy. Across his little chest: *I believe in Santa.* The letters blur. Santa wipes his eyes, gently lowers the carrier onto the sidewalk. His other hand surrenders the knife, blade tip down, to the guard who's caught up to him.

"I'm sorry about your arm," Santa says, tears again forming.

"Come on inside until the police come," she guides him with gentle hands the color of caramel.

Snooki has found her baby and is now yelling into the small gathering, "Who took my Neiman bag?"

In a former janitor's closet, the guard offers Santa her chair. He remains standing: "Please, get your arm examined. I will pay for everything."

"It's going to be okay," Carmelita says, her brown eyes brightening. She nods at a plate of macaroons, shortbread, linzer tarts and gingersnaps on her desk. "I love to bake. Help yourself."

O Holy Tart

Carmelita didn't know about Santa Claus until she was told he wasn't real. When Americans asked where she was born, she told them Casablanca. Unless they'd seen the movie or knew Casablanca was Morocco's largest city (most didn't), she'd tell them she was from a little village outside of Rabat, quickly followed by *Morocco*. They nodded as if she'd recited the viscosity of coconut oil.

Carmelita's mother was a French journalist whose work frequently took her to Northern Africa. She met a man from Mali who worked for the newly established Commonwealth Trade Union Council in 1980. Carmelita was born a year later.

By way of an elf called Black Pete, most Africans knew of Santa Claus. Carmelita's parents, however, refused to perpetuate a racist emblem of The Netherlands' and Belgium's colonial past, imported to the Dark Continent generations back.

Carmelita did not have enough time with her parents to learn why they didn't tell her fairy tales, why she didn't she go to Muslim *or* Christian schools, and why they all stayed up half the night reading and writing. She simply didn't know that she and her parents were different from other families.

She was almost 10 when they were taken from her, most likely murdered, while working on human rights for Algerian chemical workers. This much she learned from her father's sister – stern, smart, single – a highly unusual woman for her time and place who immediately moved the two of them to Paris.

It was in Paris that Carmelita, already several grades ahead of her cohorts, apprenticed with a patisserie chef and a master baker on the Left Bank.

Of course, Santa knew none of Carmelita's past, but this last bit of information would have explained why her homemade delicacies were the most heavenly he'd ever tasted. Yet, even an unabridged history of Carmelita would not have explained her immense capacity for empathy and forgiveness.

As the police arrived at the security closet door, Carmelita looked surprised and suddenly a bit nervous. The store manager, Rodney Steiger, must have driven to the other store across town, was stuck in traffic or with Milton who every employee knew was his lover.

"Is this the perpetrator?" one officer asked Carmelita.

"Officers, I appreciate you getting here so promptly. I believe Mr. Steiger is willing to drop all charges against Santa." A small lie wouldn't hurt.

Another officer noticed dried blood around a two-inch rip in Carmelita's jacket sleeve. "If that is a wound you sustained in the altercation, we have no choice." He didn't wait for her to answer.

"Let's go, sir," the officer grasped Santa's left arm.

Santa was still savoring his linzer tart, "But how do you create these?" he asked Carmelita.

"What will you do with him?" she invoked a more stern tone.

"Is this a domestic dispute?" the second officer sounded confused.

Santa blushed. Carmelita took control, "No, but if our company is not interested in pressing charges, there is no reason to use your time and resources this way."

Her logic hung like useless mistletoe in the tiny room. The officers flanked Santa who looked at Carmelita as if he'd just recognized the utility of compliance. If he did what they said, surely he'd be released in time to see her again by Christmas.

A Leftist Jolly Old Elf

Mrs. Claus was furious. "What a fool!" she'd screamed at Pinko, the unfortunate messenger of Santa's arrest, incarceration and arraignment. She'd intended to laugh sarcastically, but Miz C was a pitiful actress. *Miz C* was what she insisted the Master Crafters call her now. And Miz C desperately needed Santa to sign divorce papers ASAP.

"What about our next paycheck? End-of-year bonuses?" Pinko tried to keep his voice even.

"Are you kidding me?" Miz C laughed a throaty, dark chortle. Pinko sometimes thought that Mrs. Claus was kidnapped 15 years ago, that The Legion of Doom had cloned her and brainwashed her into... this. And by *this* she was hard to explain without a visual: an even more cartoonish yet horrifying Joan Rivers or Carrot Top—shiny sheets of skin stretched over chiseled bone and Botox filler. But even the Internet's most frightening celebrity "after" images seemed normal, comparatively.

Miz C's face and neck had been lifted so many times and so dramatically, she resembled nothing human, not even animal. Her flesh was wrenched so tightly, one could see the inside membranes of her mouth; her beady eyes embedded in a state of perpetual surprise like Joker's. Pinko couldn't believe Miz C was the same soft woman – once in both body and heart – who'd fed and burped baby elves while their parents and grandparents worked proudly.

"I got 73 percent working 20 hours OT and a third of them are working doubles everyday."

"It's called seasonal work," she said bitterly, then remembered that she might need Pinko at some point. "How about you and I go in on a good lawyer for him?"

Pinko was slow to speak. He wasn't the brightest peg on the Lite Brite board but he wasn't dim. Pinko had bettered himself, an associate degree at 67 years old and then an operations management baccalaureate at 73, all while working for The Man—Olga's moniker for Santa.

Olga, aka Big O, was indispensible during the Master Crafters' first collective bargaining contract. After Pinko's wife died, Olga further enlarged his conception of justice. He learned that capitalism and democracy rarely hold hands; to have no say in how one makes a living is serfdom; and that women should climax at least once before, during and after intercourse. She was a relentless and limber teacher.

Thanks to her tutelage, Pinko had changed for the better. Big O had reversed his Earth's rotation like Superman, made him feel like a young man luxuriating in a liberal arts program on a co-ed campus. She not only empowered the Master Crafters, she'd given Pinko the power to think and to love without restraint. With pensive gratitude, he accepted her departure back to the Ukraine. He trusted her.

Miz C was nothing like Olga. While he'd become more liberal in his attitudes about many things, including social mores, Pinko was a moral man. If married folks wanted to take lovers, that was their business. But it should be informed consent. Santa was so frazzled, so focused on how to finance another Christmas, he didn't see how Miz C flaunted her affair with Joker. And did Joker know that Miz C had thrown her scary synthetic shell at another Supervillain? Green Goblin took her for an overnight spin in his glider just last week.

"We have very little in our dues fund, almost enough to help cover Itchy's co-pay for his hemorrhoid operation. It's up for a vote next week."

Miz C laughed as if this were hilarious.

Pinko told her that he had to get back to work.

"You think about how badly you need Santa out of the slammer. Instead of covering your comrade's ass – pun intended – you should be thinking about your own."

And with that, Pinko left the room, feeling unmoored, less confident and sorely missing Olga.

Not Even a Mouse

Olga has returned to Kiev, to Sergey as promised. Olga is nothing if not a woman of her word. Almost three years of North Pole memories so sharp and crystallized two weeks ago now thaw under grey skies, longer lines and an economy that isn't built to make people smile.

Ah, Pinko. Her old, widower elf man who surprised her myriad times. In myriad ways. Ah, her *myshka*, her little grey mouse. He knew she couldn't stay; Sergey had approved her extension three times. A fourth was impossible. Sergey needed her. He would soon send her to the next revolution.

At Boryspil International Airport, she watches the state news on a small monitor outside Sergey's gate. She sees The Man inside a jail cell. The crawler reads *New Jersey. Awaiting trial. Attempted theft and armed assault.* Pinko must be frantic! Why hasn't he called?

Olga hears the PA announce Sergey's arrival. She will hold herself together and pretend for him tonight. She will make a magnificent display of unbounded lust and affection. She will redefine lover. She will turn up the heat, melt all remaining shards of North Pole memories and bind her heart, a heart that bleeds pink and grey.

Dear Deranged Santa

The media had its fun. Bill Hader developed a *Dear Deranged Santa* character. Naturally, Bobby Moynihan played Snooki and Maya Rudolf guest starred as Carmelita on SNL. Santa was spared few parodies. Some were cruel. Bill O'Reilly blamed Obamacare.

Not that Santa had access to any electronics. Not that he would have turned any of it on. But the mail poured in. Most of it from lawyers seeking a remake of *Miracle on 34th Street*, starring them. Santa left those unopened. But he couldn't refuse reading letters from everyone else, even if his address was now State Prison, Trenton, NJ.

Carmelita had lost her job. Actually she returned it to Rodney Steiger, who had come back after a vigorous afternoon with Milton in the backroom of his store across town, screaming obscenities as he pounded on the security closet door. She opened it, his balled fist mid-air, and told him that he could "take this job and shove it, which should be no problem for you."

Carmelita instantly regretted adding those last few words. She was not a hater, certainly not a homophobe, but was at that moment not her centered, kind self. Rodney was a blamer, a privileged unhappy man who told ethnic and sexist jokes intended to keep his 'girls and boys', many of them twice his age, in their places. He gave LGBT a bad name.

Rodney stood there, arm still raised, open-mouthed as she continued, "I'm giving my two-week notice which includes 17 unused sick, emergency, personal and vacation days." She placed a hand-written letter in his unraised hand and walked sideways out the small door, past his statue.

Sweet Bribe O' Mine

Carmelita drives to the prison every day. The first two days her visits are refused. The third day she brings some linzer tarts and peanut butter-chocolate mousse and is lucky enough to find a young man with a kind face at the gate. She explains her predicament: she needs to give Santa his holistic tinctures for gout. Even the young man named Martin who resembles a young Danny Glover sees her struggle with this lie.

She stops herself mid-sentence. "Oh, here it is, Martin. Sergeant. Officer Martin? I'm sorry. I have been refused for the last two days and I would like nothing more than to see Santa, to give him comfort."

Martin sees her earnestness. She lowers her window all the way down and his mouth waters from what's wafting from boxes in the front passenger seat.

"If you don't arrest me for attempted bribery, I'd like to give you a gift." She opens the top box and pulls out a generous ramekin of mousse along with two tarts. Martin's hands involuntarily meet hers at the window. He tells her to wait, disappears into the guard hut and two minutes later the heavy arm of the blockade lifts. As she inches forward, Martin hands her a visitor badge from the hut's sliding window and says, "All clear, ma'am. These are the most delicious things I've ever tasted!"

With a smile, Carmelita sails inside the prison.

Santa's Handlers

Pinko was not the only one worried about Santa, Miz C notwithstanding. He'd managed to steer clear of her since she'd asked him to pay half of Santa's defense. Pinko would not make a deal with the devil's devil. Itchy needed his operation. His children and wife were down to their last can of beans. The Master Crafters' vote had been virtually unanimous: Help Itchy. One new guy named Peter Boyd had voted no.

Although the Master Crafters exchanged gifts and made merry, the prospect of losing Christmas was about losing their economy. Like Inuits losing whales and caribou. One could only get so sentimental about starving, regardless of culture. Olga knew this like the back of her empty hand, when growing up in Russia.

Santa rubbed his eyes when Olga appeared on the other side of the bars. "Yes," she said, "It's me." Intuiting his next question, she answered: "I have come to help and you must… I should say you *should* believe me."

"The world is upside down," was all Santa said before he spilled everything he could remember: the layaway line, his growing debt, sweating in the artificial heat, surrounded by incivility and narcissistic whining. He told Olga how his brain seemed to leave his body as he witnessed his leg bend at the knee "And *pow!* as if it had been spring-loaded."

As Olga suppressed a smile and scribbled her last notes, a guard accompanied Carmelita – arms full of mostly-empty boxes (Americans fooled themselves that their culture didn't thrive on bribery, she mused) – to Santa's cell. The two women looked at one another with detached curiosity.

Santa introduced Olga to … "Oh, dear," he said and bowed his head. "This beautiful new friend and I don't even know her name."

Olga recognized that this woman was the security guard who'd implored New Jersey's finest to release Santa. "It's Carmelita. Carmelita Touré. Carmelita extended her hand.

Santa softly said, "Of course it is."

Olga politely refused one of Carmelita's boxed treasures and the guard, a short, balding man, begged one more. Carmelita asked if she would be granted a visit tomorrow and he assured her she would as his Vienna sausage-like fingers reached for another mousse.

Santa extended his hand outside the bars. "Carmelita, Carmelita." After placing her boxes on the chair vacated by Olga, Carmelita took his hand and a sweetness not known in the culinary or philanthropic worlds ran through both of their bodies. Neither could have said whether their shared slice of heaven lasted seconds or minutes, but each felt it so intensely that something like nirvana began to replace their sense of separateness. Carmelita was the one to reluctantly withdraw her hand.

She showed him the wound, healing well under sterile gauze. After she re-taped it and rolled down her sleeve, Santa put the pads of his fingers to his lips and placed them gently atop the injury for which he was responsible. She smiled and opened a box. Santa took two tarts and a mousse, saving the last ramekin for an officer she might meet on her way out.

They talked about Morocco and Paris, about the sad state of education and entertainment. They even spoke easily about love and how necessary yet tragic it can be when people change. And finally, Santa told Carmelita that Olga had a plan.

Red and Green

Sergey Khorkov enjoyed Olga's welcome home gift, knowing there would be a request once he was happily and utterly spent. He'd known for several months that his number one field agent and longtime paramour had allowed herself to fall for a feeble elf. That knowledge, acquired by a new recruit – Peter Boyd – both repulsed and energized him.

Sergey had no fantasies of monogamy between himself and Olga. She had taught him more about lovemaking when she was barely 18 than he was ever capable of reciprocating. Two decades later, now well into in his fifties, he knew that man didn't create earthquakes, that a woman's tectonic plates shifted to her own magic. A man could only facilitate the release of her rupture and, with practice, help extend its duration. All women were born with this magic, but women like Olga were not afraid to exploit it, to conjure every carnal atom into seismic flows that sounded like the Earth dancing to its swan song.

But loyalty was another matter. He demanded it. His repulsion had less to do with Pinko's age and stature than with Olga's omissions. After three years, no mention of her affection for Pinko. *Deceit!* Sergey's energy came from what would now be a game. If Olga could hide her true intentions – saving Santa to help her beloved – then she didn't need to know that Sergey would make her work more difficult.

Thanks to the fat little bald man at NJ State Prison, he had an audio file of Olga and Santa's conversation. He also had surveillance photos, two blurry but one crisp, of the lovely Carmelita Touré.

"Now there's a woman who's not afraid," he said, touching himself.

He's a Mean One, Mr. Grinch

The Joker is mellowing. That's what he tells himself. The ancient past, acid under the bridge, an accidental transformation that actually fit his bad-ass persona. Now, he has an accomplice who appears to have had the same accident but her vanity has blinded her. Miz C thinks she's beautiful, he sniggers.

Love is surely blind. Only Joker wouldn't know and he's at peace with that.

Once Santa signs the divorce papers, the old witch will get half the Iceberg, half of bloody Christmas. Then after a quick trip to Vegas, the pronouncement of Joker and wife, he will own it all—even what's left of Christmas spirit.

December 25th will soon end up where it's been headed all along: One big joke.

His iPhone buzzes. Miz C doesn't want to bother him, but she's unable to come up with enough liquidity to hire the legal team her husband needs to get back to work.

"Why don't you empty the midgets' 401k?"

Over her objections, he simply says, "Yes. Yes you can. A few phone calls. Or put Pinkey-Dinkey under duress."

23

The dumb bitch hadn't thought of that.

"Uh, huh. Love you, too," he ends the call, turns off his phone.

Before Joker leaves to shoot a new commercial featuring chemical peels in tropical scents and designer colors, he scans his email and spots a familiar name. "Sergey Khorkov," he chants, "Commie jerk-off."

Dirty Santa Gift Exchange

Before Pinko's wife died, before Mrs. Claus lost that first fateful pound, even before Olga was a gleam in her father's eye, Carmelita's father learned the underbelly of capitalism in a Cornell University classroom. An international labor policy class during his U.S. year abroad that abruptly ended his enthusiasm for Western finance. His professor passed around two photos of Jack Jesterson—the first his Acme Chemical Company ID, and the second what was left of his face after the accident. Eight other more fortunate casualties had died, their families paid millions to keep their lips together. Jack had escaped from a state hospital and was presumed dead.

When Carmelita's father met her mother, he confided his spiritual transformation in that Cornell classroom. His palpable compassion and his eagerness to do good in the world conspired to loosen her mother's blouse, unzip her skirt and take all of his goodness into her.

Like Carmelita's father, Sergey Khorkov sought a more just world. Their conception of justice, however, was incongruent. Sergey knew of Jack Jesterson's plight thanks to Amerikos willing to put personal profiteering over patriotism during the Cold War. (*And they think their bread is not buttered with grease*, he was fond of saying.) In fact, it was the KGB who found Jesterson and transported his barely breathing remains to Belarus where his disintegrated face was transformed into something less horrifying by the Soviet Bloc's best surgeons.

During Jesterson's convalescence, Sergey took many opportunities to chat with him ("Please, call me Joker," he would chuckle) about America and its cult of capitalism. Over six months of recovery, Joker seemed less concerned about his still repugnant yet cartoonish features and more interested in Sergey's thoughts. Could any government, any system that depended upon servitude, sacrifice, and trust, be trusted?

Sergey read him the Complete Works of Lenin, Stalin, an up-and-comer named Gorbachev, and for pleasure, Dostoyevsky and Tolstoy. Joker learned to speak Mother Russian with some fluency. They spoke of the future, of justice, and Joker's rightful place in the world. Three weeks before he was discharged, Joker agreed to resurface as the Soviet Union's greatest weapon: The Face of America.

The day Joker was released from the sanatorium, Sergey handed him keys to a lavish flat. "The driver is waiting for you. We'll dine tonight before leaving for Moscow," he hugged his comrade, although it was always difficult to lean in to something that unnatural.

Joker smiled – but he always did and that in itself took some getting used to – and accepted the keys. When Sergey arrived at the flat later that evening, Joker and the car were gone, the driver dead under the bushes.

Epiphany

On Christmas Day, 1991, the Soviet flag waved over Moscow's Kremlin for the last time. Olga remembered Gorbachev's farewell, her father dying of cirrhosis, his mind still sharp as a Siberian storm, telling her, "History repeats itself, human nature rarely changes and love blinds." Olga had forgotten his admonition that day at the prison—until the short, bald guard who escorted her from Santa's cell to the door began to fidget with a black dot on his collar. Sergey's mole.

Olga exited the gates, bought a cheap phone and got Pinko's sad hello on the fourth ring.

"Myshka!"

Pinko's face beamed. Although she couldn't see them, she imagined his beautiful wrinkles lifting up, igniting his green eyes as he smiled. He began to confess how much he missed her, but she had to interrupt. "Listen, my love, I have little time."

So Pinko listened, trying to block out his desires at the sound of his beloved, learning more about Santa's story, and most importantly, Sergey's surveillance of Olga and its implications.

"Tell me, Myshka, tell me what the old bat is up to."

Pinko told her about Miz C's proposal to pay half of Santa's counsel. Then how, just two hours ago, he was notified that the union's retirement account password had been changed.

"The stuffed scarecrow!" she said in Russian. "So, she wants the divorce papers signed immediately. And we all know she does whatever The Madman wants." It took Olga a few seconds to put the pixels in place. A recognizable picture was forming.

Of course! Joker would attempt the first holiday hostile takeover. But, why would Sergey have her every word taped? If he were jealous (*which he wasn't, was he?*) he could easily have her tailed, her whereabouts and a few photos forwarded. No, Sergey wanted to know her strategy to save Santa in order to thwart her efforts. Was Sergey in cahoots with Joker? A double spy?

Olga wasted no more time except to tell Pinko that she would be with him soon. "And one more thing: you need to go Lilliputian on Miz C's ass. Get your strongest comrades, use indestructible – Olga's pronunciation of that word was almost as good as feeling her thighs against his small crumpled face – restraints. And tie that bitch down."

Olga explained to Carmelita what they were up against. "The Legion of Doom is always doomed. Too many bad egos."

"As in the waffle?" Carmelita asked.

"As in men's egos are always too big, but when you pour evil syrup all over them, the men can never share for long."

Carmelita caught enough of Olga's metaphor, hopefully.

Olga went on: "So, we use evil to fight evil, no?"

Carmelita would do whatever Olga suggested. Olga was a spitfire, a Slavic Joan of Arc, a girl who made *The Girl with the Dragon Tattoo* look like *Hello Kitty*. Of course, her accent heightened her credibility.

"Why don't you elucidate." Carmelita suggested.

"Out of all Legion members, Joker not play well with others," when Olga got this excited, she slipped in and out of her native syntax. "I know this. Personally."

Carmelita raised her eyebrows.

"Before Sergey, before growing up—I thought I'd like to… be… how you say… sidestep?"

"Sidekick? To Joker?"

"Yes to sidekick. No to Joker. I train under Lex Luthor. As far as bad guys go, class act." And she swept her hands away from her lithe body to emphasize Luthor's position in the villain hierarchy. Apparently, no one came close.

"What happened?"

"Two things. One, I attended Legion of Doom meetings with Lex. Documented everything on my own devices. If not caught – they had rules of no recording – then I'd know my device was pretty good. Stealth. Anyway, I saw firsthand how difficult Joker was. He trusted no one and many good plan fail because of him."

"What's the other thing?" Carmelita suddenly wanted popcorn and a movie seat.

"Thing two: Sergey come along. Less violence. Better health benefits."

Carmelita laughed, then turned serious. "Weren't you afraid? All those maniacs in the same room?"

Olga mirrored Carmelita's solemnity. "Here is where I differ from most—both men and women. Yes, I fear. But I fear most of all stupidity. Mistakes, accidents, being unprepared. Most villains in the Legion not stupid. Just big waffles."

Oogie Boogie

Joker read Sergey's electronic missive as his cold heart fluttered with something like joy. "Now, he wants me again!" Joker said aloud, "This must be good."

He didn't hit reply, but picked up a black stationary phone, punched in a string of numbers and said slowly and clearly in Russian, "Comrade, we have a deal." Then he laid the receiver in its cradle, raked through his green hair, straightened his tie in the mirror and left for his commercial.

Dynamic Duo and the Legion of Doom

Carmelita was stunning. Olga had worked up profiles on The Legion of Doom members, their strengths, likes, dislikes and Achilles heels. With Olga's computer-like brain and Carmelita's intelligence, poise and beauty, this could work.

Thanks to Olga's hacking skills, the likes of which were unknown to anyone except maybe Sergey, Carmelita was standing before the Legion, in the middle of a cave. The pooled water reflected against stalagmites that in turn, bathed her in soft light. But instead of looking like herself, an angel, she was dressed in iridescent eggplant: almost black but for purple sparks. She was at once the epitome of beauty and danger—irresistible to everyone in the Legion, especially Luthor.

"So what you'd like us to do is turn on our brother, Joker," Captain Cold said.

"If by turn on you mean obstruct his attempts, then yes." Olga had instructed her to never allow emotion to throw her. The Legion was famous in its use of pretense, for presenting emotional arguments as a test of others' strength. Strength equaled power and power was always destroyed by emotion.

"Look around you. A quorum. But who's missing?" Carmelita asked authoritatively.

"We control our own schedules. Your insolence is both disturbing and brave," Luthor said.

"My insolence, courage or humility is irrelevant, with due respect. I am here to ask for your assistance, and in so doing, to compensate your efforts."

"Proceed," Luthor said, trying to ignore her body, a classic fifties pin up with real curves and class, her native culture a mystery which turned him on even more.

With superb elocution, the dark princess detailed their reward: possession of Joker's strategic and tactical plans aimed to vanquish the Legion, member by member, until he alone reigned Supreme Evildoer; the early release of at least 1,000 criminals in New Jersey – fresh recruits for the Legion – and Christmas gifts. Santa would take them off the naughty list for as long as they lived.

Solomon Grundy squealed. Toyman openly wept.

"We'll have to convene privately," Luthor tried to retain some semblance of order.

"Of course. I'll wait outside," Carmelita bowed. "As a token of appreciation, I hope you will accept my gifts." And on cue, the Legion's security guards – who predictably devoured the fourth tray when she arrived – wheeled in three carts, all lined with St. Lucia buns, rum baba cake, cruller angel wings, banana pecan dacquoise, orange trifle with Grand Marnier, caramel-cloaked chocolate-hazelnut torte, gingerbread pear trifle, peppermint chocolate cheesecake and, of course, linzer tarts.

Run Run Rudolf

When the walls came down at State Prison, Santa was fast asleep. He thought he was dreaming: airlifted by Superman. But it was Bizarro who cradled Santa and set him down on his native ice.

Olga thought about the Berlin Wall, her early ambivalence followed by hope. Through binoculars from a high tree branch in a playground a few blocks away, Olga watched newly-freed New Jerseyans, some innocent, others guilty of heinous crimes, emerge from the blast, some jumping up and down, others running toward the Legion's line of stretch limos. Luthor knows how to treat recruits, she thought, *a real class act*.

Lex Luthor received all pass codes to Joker's files, servers, classified clouds—the most incriminating evidence fabricated and time stamped by Olga. Enough data to keep Joker in harm's way for another decade or more.

Most of the world, those who rule no one, control nothing but perhaps their reactions to ubiquitous reports of social, spiritual and financial doom, were happy to see the old guy break free. Even Santa's court-appointed lawyers who never got their 15 minutes of fame, let out a collective breath of relief.

Snooki screamed a few obscenities.

Epilogue: Love Actually

Love always chooses the same identity: anonymous superhero. Its kryptonite causes temporary blindness but love's full, unleashed force more than compensates for its shadowy short-sighted effects the moment one person commits to it.

He or she only needs to believe. Then come the miracles.

Christmas happened. Santa wrapped his letter of apology with leather-bound editions of *The Brothers Karamazov*, *The Master and Margarita*, *Anna Karenina*, *Crime and Punishment* and *The Idiot*. Snooki now dreams of dancing in Red Square.

Carmelita's company, Universal Love Goods, grossed several billion in its first year. Enough to help Santa pay off his debts and launch a nonprofit to feed people with meat, vegetables and fruit—no added sugar. With Oprah's help, they raised more money for decent roads, schools, and hospitals in third world countries. When she's not on the road or in the air, Carmelita likes to experiment in and outside of the kitchen with Santa. They only taste-test together.

Before marrying Pinko, Olga returned to Kiev to say goodbye to Sergey. He was already gone. She wanted to tell him that she'd had no choice. Perhaps he'd felt the same way when he learned that she was in love with Pinko. Olga would rather believe Sergey had gone soft, had wanted her exclusively, than to imagine he'd cast his lot with a capitalist pig like Joker.

And Joker? He and Miz C are under the knife again. Trying to blend into mainstream, that's the plan according to their texts and calls, so easy to hack that Olga does it as she watches *Extreme Home Makeover*. Every once in awhile, Olga feels a twinge of empathy: *mainstream life; how boring!* Then she realizes she is curled up on a La-Z-Boy sofa, Pinko's soft corrugated face in her lap, weeping. She whispers to her beloved, "Myshka, could I be pregnant?"